Published by Simply Read Books 2006. Text © Sara O'Leary. Illustrations © Julie Morstad. 5432 All rights reserved. No part of this publication may be reproduced, stored in a retrieval system, or transmitted, in any form or by any means, electronic, mechanical, photocopying, recording or otherwise, without the written permission of the publisher. CIP available from Library and Archives Canada. We gratefully acknowledge the support of the Canada Council for the Arts and the BC Arts Council for our publishing program. Color separations by ScanLab. Design by Robin Mitchell for hundreds & thousands design inc. Third printing.

When You Were Small

Sara O'Leary

Pictures by Julie Morstad

Simply Read Books

Every night at bedtime Henry and his father
have a chat.

It always begins the same way.

"Dad," says Henry.

"Tell me about when I was small."

When you were small you used to have a pet ant and you would take him out for walks on a leash.

When you were small we used you as a chess piece, because our chess board was missing one of the knights and you were the perfect size.

When you were small we used to give you baths in the teapot, and when you were done we could just tip it over and pour you out.

When you were small we let you sleep in one of my slippers. The left one. You used a fuzzy wash cloth for a blanket and a tea bag for a pillow.

When you were small your mother once
lost you in the bottom of her purse.

When she found you again, you were clinging
to an earring she'd lost three years before.

When you were small you wore a thimble
for a hat.

When you were small you rode on the cat's back like you were an emperor and he was an elephant.

When you were small you used a ruler
for a toboggan.

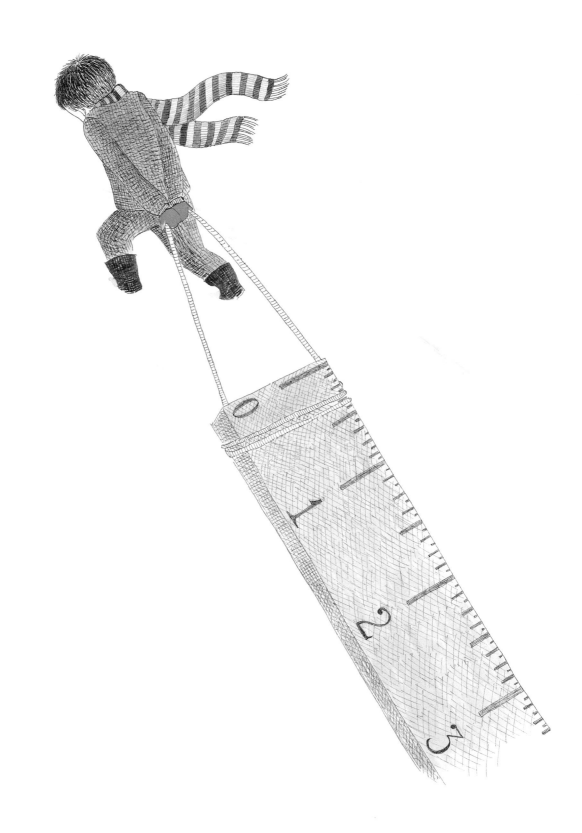

When you were small we put you on the top of the Christmas tree instead of the angel.

When you were small you couldn't hold a spoon so you used to sit on the edge of my porridge bowl and dip your head in like a baby bird.

When you were small we brushed your hair
with a toothbrush.

*W*hen you were small we took the toy castle out of the aquarium and you were king of it.

When you were small, I used to carry you around in the pocket of my shirt. Your little head would just stick out and your little hands would grip onto the edge of the cloth. Actually you ripped a lot of my shirts that way.

VVhen you were small," says his dad, "we wanted to call you Hieronymous but it was too big a name for you and so we shortened it to Henry."

"Dad," says Henry, "is all that true?"

"Well," says his dad, "don't you remember?"

THE END

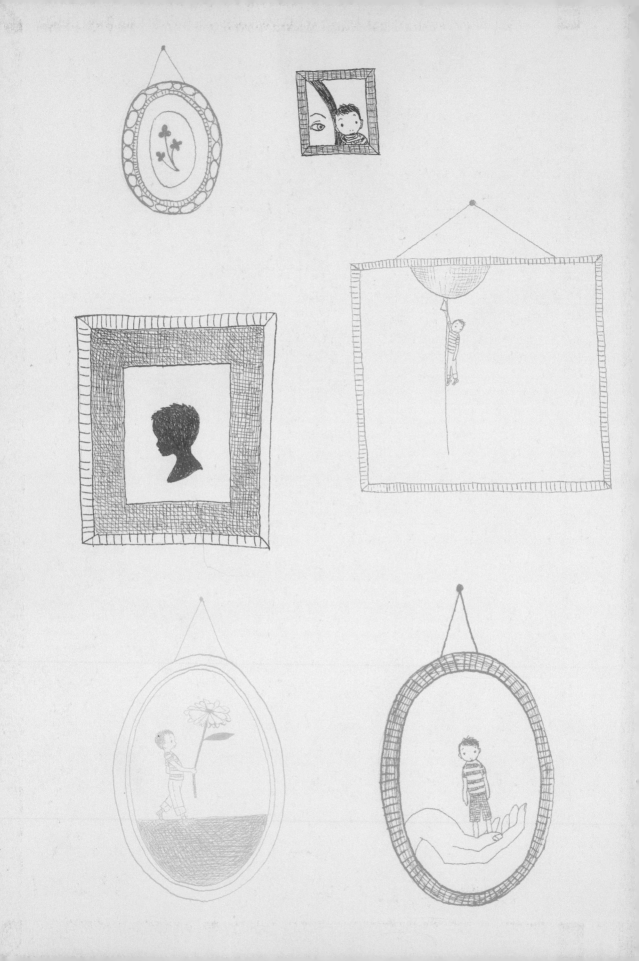